Dial Books for Young Readers • an imprint of Penguin Group (USA) Inc.

Jon Agee
Little Santa

In the North Pole, in a little cabin, lived Mr. and Mrs. Claus and their seven children, Larry, Mary, Willy, Millie, Joey, Zoe, and Santa.

Life was tough in the North
Pole. Every day, there was
more wood to be chopped,

more snow to be shoveled,

another fish to be caught,

a quilt to be mended,

and a fire to be stoked.

The Clauses were miserable!

Except for Santa. He *loved* the North Pole.
He liked making snow angels, and snowmen,

decorating pine trees,

and baking gingerbread cookies
in the shape of people.

Most of all, he liked sliding down the chimney.

So, when the Clauses decided to move to Florida, Santa was very sad.

"Won't you miss all the pine trees and the icicles and the miles and miles of snow?"

"No, Santa," they said, "we won't."

That night, as everyone packed,
there was a terrible blizzard.

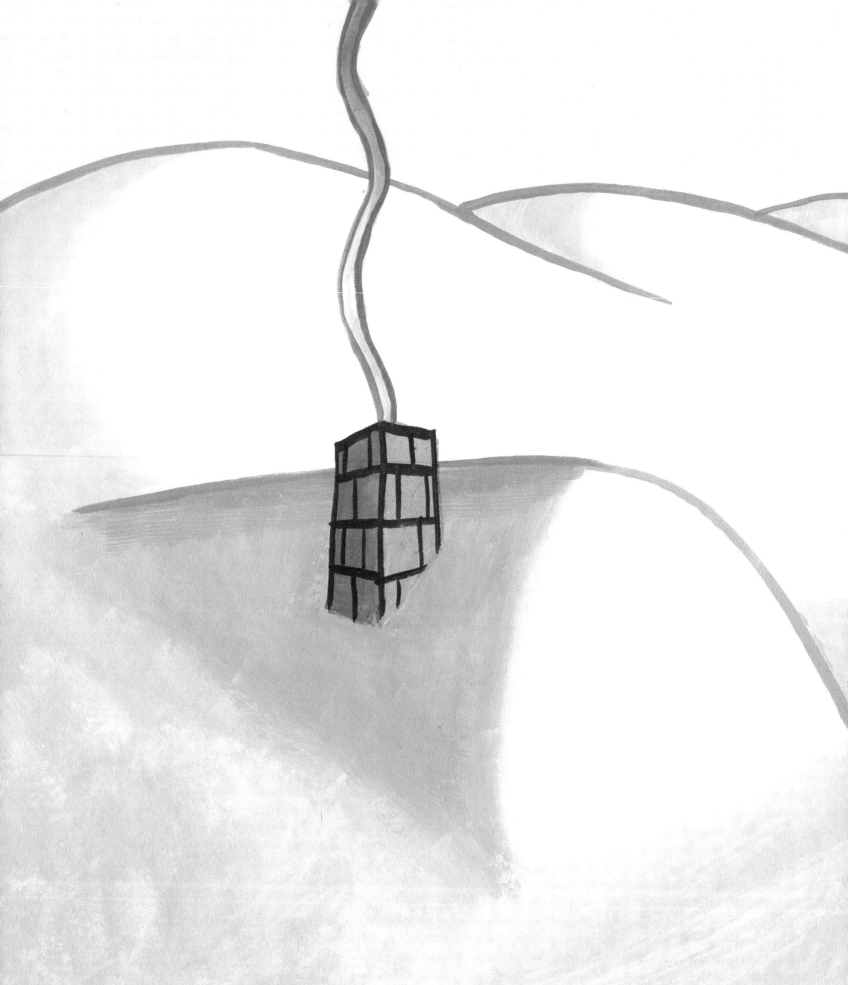

The next morning, the house was buried under a huge snow drift. The Clauses were trapped.

"What are we going to do?" said Mrs. Claus.
"I know!" said Santa. "I can shimmy up the chimney!"

So Mr. and Mrs. Claus gave Santa some food, and some snow shoes, and sent him to get help.

After a long walk he came to a little branch.

"Ho, ho, ho," said Santa. "You must be the top of a tall tree."

"No," said a voice, "I'm a very c-c-cold reindeer."

Santa dug the reindeer out of the snow.

"G-g-gosh!" said the reindeer. "What are you doing out here?"

Santa told the reindeer about his family.

"Hop on my back," said the reindeer. "We'll look for help."

"Gee whiz!" said Santa. "You're a pretty special reindeer."

On a tall bluff, they saw a house. A light was on inside.
"Stop here," said Santa.
The reindeer landed, and Santa slid down the chimney.

The house was full of elves.

"Holy snowflake!" said the oldest one. "Who are you?"

Santa introduced himself and told the elves about his family.

"We can help," said the elf. "We'll make shovels so we can dig them out of the snow!"

In no time at all, the shovels were made.

"Now, Santa," said the elf, "how will we get to your house?"

"I've got a flying reindeer," said Santa.

"Wow!" said the elf. "And do you have a sleigh too?"

"What's a sleigh?" said Santa.

"Well, well!" said the elf. "I guess we'll build you one!"

The next morning, it was finished.
Santa hooked up the reindeer,
and everybody climbed aboard.
"Ready?" said the reindeer.
"Ready," said Santa.
Off they went, to look
for Santa's house.

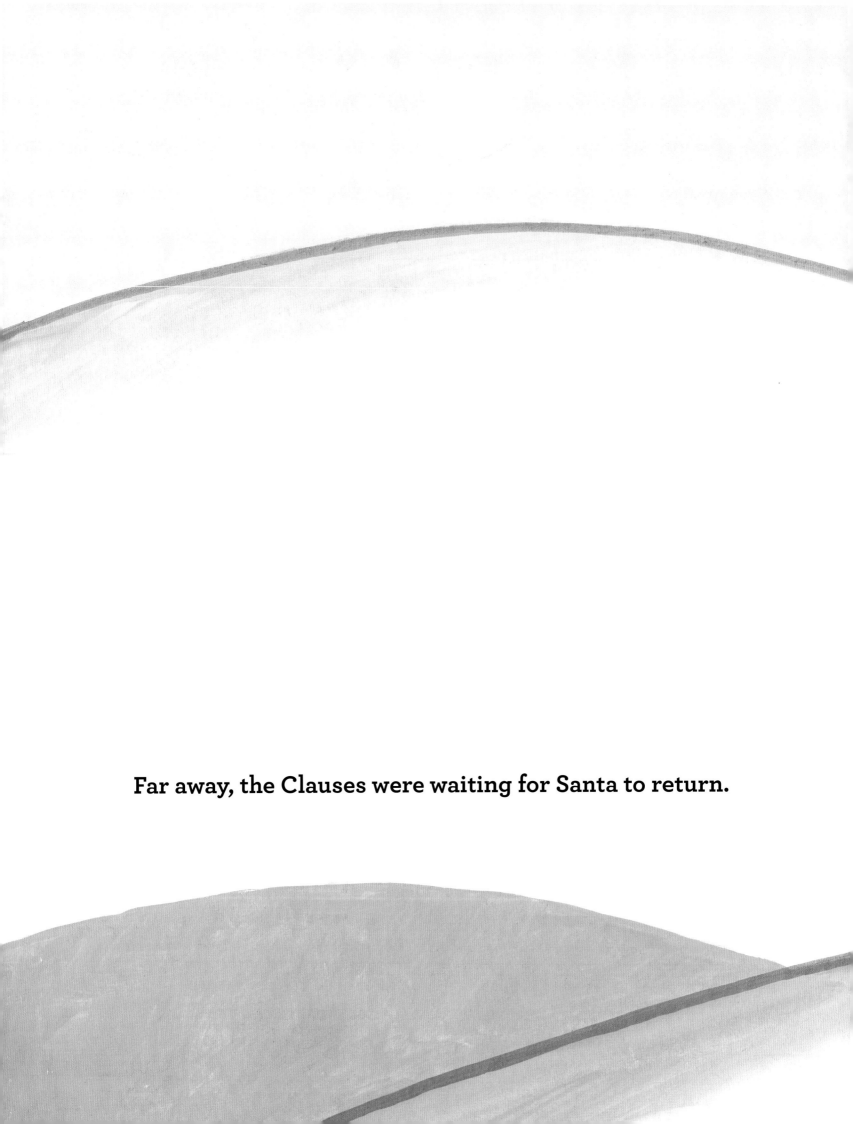

Far away, the Clauses were waiting for Santa to return.

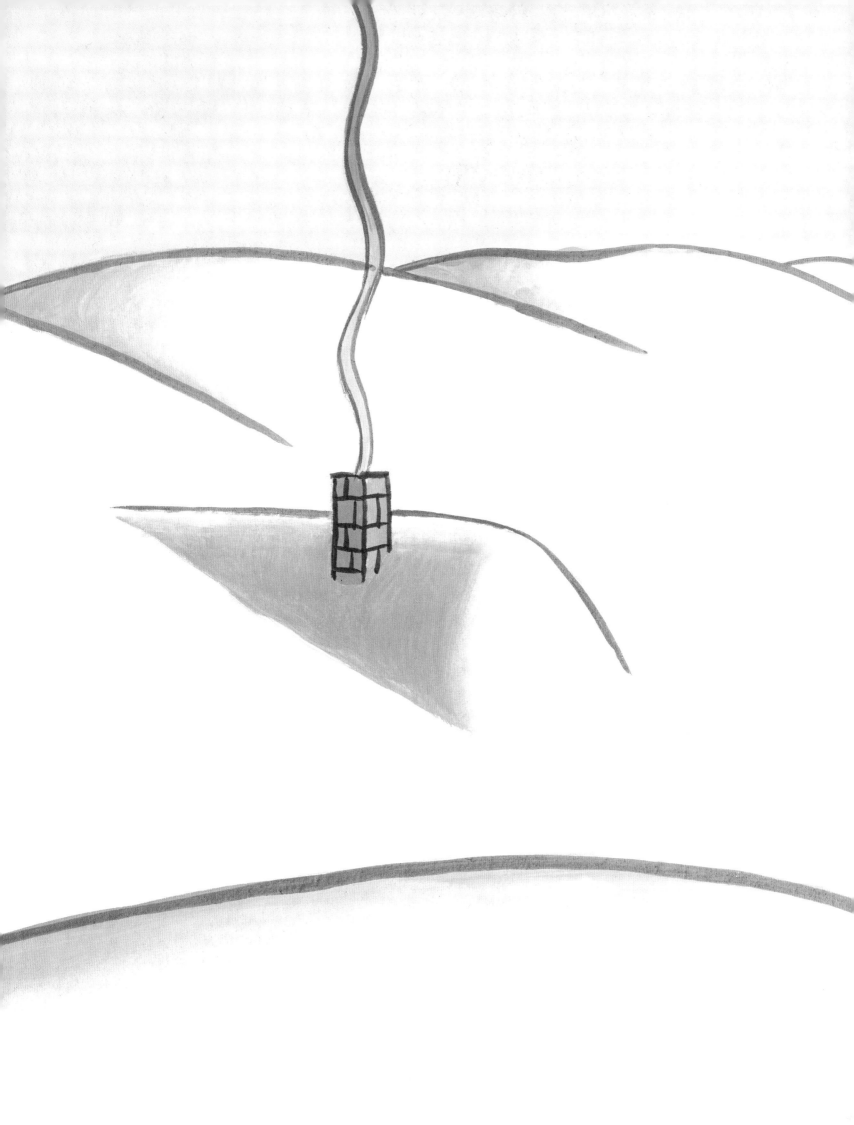

It was almost midnight when the dog heard
a familiar noise coming from the chimney.
Could it be—?

"Ho, ho, ho!" said Santa. "I'm home!"
The Clauses were overjoyed.
But there was *more* noise, coming from just outside.
Santa opened the door.

"Look, everybody!" said Santa. "These are my new friends!"
"Welcome," said Santa's family.

Well, it was a good year in the North Pole. The
Clauses and the elves spent lots of time together,
and life wasn't as tough as it was before.

But when winter came, Santa's family decided to move to Florida after all.

Santa? He stayed behind.

And you know the rest of the story.

DIAL BOOKS FOR YOUNG READERS
A division of Penguin Young Readers Group • Published by The Penguin Group
Penguin Group (USA) Inc., 375 Hudson Street, New York, NY 10014, U.S.A.

USA | Canada | UK | Ireland | Australia | New Zealand | India | South Africa | China
Penguin Books Ltd, Registered Offices: 80 Strand, London WC2R 0RL, England

For more information about the Penguin Group visit penguin.com

Library of Congress Cataloging-in-Publication Data • Agee, Jon, author, illustrator. • Little Santa / Jon Agee. • pages cm •
Summary: A resident of the North Pole with the ability to slide up and down chimneys meets a flying reindeer and some
industrious elves, in this fictional biography of Santa Claus. • ISBN 978-0-8037-3906-2 (hardcover) • 1. Santa Claus—
Juvenile fiction. [1. Santa Claus—Fiction.] I. Title. • PZ7.A266Li 2013 • [E]—dc23 • 2012031855

Manufactured in China on acid-free paper
3 5 7 9 10 8 6 4 2

Designed by Lily Malcom • Text set in Archer